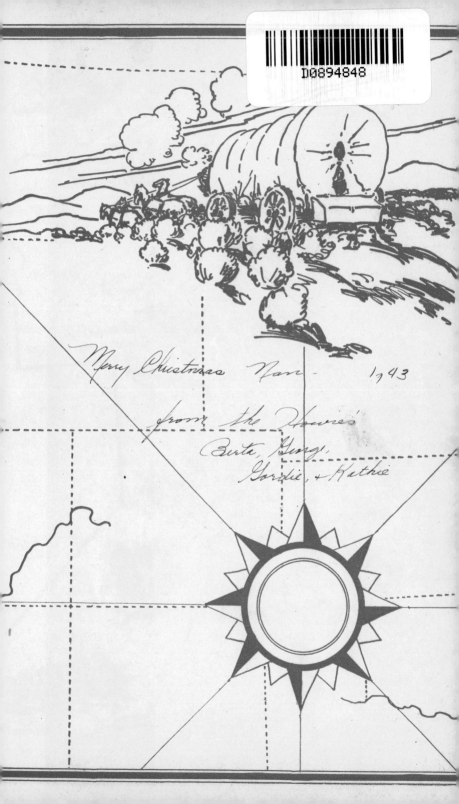

Merry Christmas Nan—   1943

from the Howie's
Berta, Ginge,
Gordie, & Kathie

CARMEN OF THE
GOLDEN COAST

CRATER LAKE, CRATER LAKE NATIONAL PARK,
SOUTHERN OREGON

CARMEN OF THE GOLDEN COAST

BY
MADELINE BRANDEIS

Photographic Illustrations

GROSSET & DUNLAP
PUBLISHERS   NEW YORK

DEDICATION

To Aunt Elsa, Beautiful and Constant,
like her Beloved Lake Tahoe.

THOSE WHO POSED FOR THE ILLUSTRATIONS IN "CARMEN OF THE GOLDEN COAST"

Carmen............................MARILYN KNOWLDEN
Mr. Stevens.........................KENNETH RANDALL
Carmencita..........................MANUELITA ORTIZ
Juan...............................ARMANDO NAVARRO
Hipolito...........................SALVADOR SOUFFLE

MARILYN is a clever little girl, who acts in motion pictures. You have, no doubt, seen her on the screen.

KENNETH has played many parts on the stage and screen and is one of the leading actors in that great spectacle of the Hollywood Hills—The Pilgrimage Play. He is so versatile that he can be a young boy one minute, and an old grandfather the next!

MANUELITA, ARMANDO, and SALVADOR live near Olvera Street, the Mexican street in Los Angeles which you will hear about when you read this story. They are real Mexican children, which means that they are affectionate, respectful and courteous. They dance the "Harabe," love music, and Mexican beans!

Thank you, my friends, for the privilege of photographing you and using your pictures in this book!

MADELINE BRANDEIS

PREFACE

This is the story of two little girls,
Each of them living in different worlds,
One in the old world, and one in the new,
One like your great-grand'ma,
One just like you.

This, also, is the story of "three big states."

You see, Marie (who is my manager, thirteen-years old, and very strict!) decided that I should write some stories about American children while we are resting between foreign journeys.

Since we came back from visiting "Tony of Italy," Marie and I met "Carmen of the Golden Coast." We think her land is about as interesting as any land we know. But then, it is our land, too, so perhaps we are not fair judges.

Some day we shall write a book about "Little You of Your State," but in the meanwhile why don't you write and tell us what part of the United States you live in? Marie and I always like to hear from the friends of our story people because we consider them our friends, too.

PREFACE

In this book we present "The Golden-Evergreen-Beaver" country. Why do I call it that? Because these three beautiful Pacific States are "Golden California," "Busy Beaver Oregon," and "Evergreen Washington."

So, a happy journey with Carmen along the Golden Coast!

Marie's

Madeline Brandeis

CONTENTS

CARMENCITA OF
YESTERDAY

CARMEN OF TODAY

TWO LITTLE GIRLS OF THE GOLDEN COAST

CARMEN OF THE GOLDEN COAST

CHAPTER I

CARMEN—TODAY

Carmen's home stood upon one of the prettiest streets in Los Angeles. Surrounding it were palm trees and velvety lawns.

But lately, Carmen's father, John Stevens, wore a frown because he was worried about a sign. This is the sign—$.

Carmen's mother, Mrs. Stevens, also had troubles which might be explained by a sign —℞. Have you ever seen it on medicine bottles? It means that the doctor has been there.

The doctor often visited Mrs. Stevens, but many people said that she only "enjoyed poor health."

Carmen Stevens was a little girl who had

11

always had everything she wanted. Most of the time she was happy and looked like the mask of comedy—☺.

But this morning Carmen woke up resembling tragedy—☹. There was a deep frown on her forehead.

"Happy birthday!" called her father outside her bedroom door.

She had almost forgotten that it was her birthday. She felt certain that it would not be a happy one. How could it be? She was not going to have a party. Perhaps she would not even receive a present!

Everything had suddenly changed. It was a sad world for Carmen Stevens. Father had lost his position. They had been obliged to sell their home and were soon to move away. They were going to Seattle, a city in a state called Washington, to live with a very old grand-aunt. Leaving friends. Leaving beautiful California!

Carmen turned her head toward the wall

and began to cry. Her father entered the room and sat down by her bed. He took her hand.

"What is the matter, little birthday girl?" he asked. "Tears today may mean tears all the year, you know."

"Oh, Daddy!" There came a muffled sob. "I don't want to go away! I don't want to leave my friends and go to Seattle to live with that . . . that old Tia!" ("Tia" means "Aunt" in Spanish.)

Tia was Great Grand-Aunt Carmencita Estevan, father's only living relative. Father had a deep family feeling for Tia. He had even named Carmen after her.

But Carmen was not proud of an old Spanish woman whom she had never met. She dreaded going to live in her home.

"Oh, why did she invite us to come?" wailed Carmen. "I don't like her! I don't!"

"Hush, my dear," said Mr. Stevens. "She is kind and is trying to help us in our trouble.

"I WONT GO!" CARMEN CRIED

She has offered to share her home with us and to help me find work in Seattle."

Carmen suddenly sat up in bed. Her cheeks were pink. Her eyes flashed. She had her mother's pale, blond beauty and golden hair. But her dark eyes reminded everyone that her father was Spanish.

John Stevens, Carmen's father, belonged

to the old Estevan family of California. "Estevan" is Spanish for "Stevens."

Carmen now began to beat the bed clothes with her fists.

"I won't go! I won't! I won't!" she cried.

"Come, my dear," said her father. "I am sure you will love Tia."

"I will not love her!" screamed Carmen. "I don't want to live in her old house! It smells of garlic! And I won't eat peppers that burn holes in my stomach! Oh!"

She hid her head and sobbed.

"You dear, stupid little goose!" laughed Mr. Stevens, patting her head. "Whoever has been telling you such things? Look! I have brought you a present."

At this magic word, Carmen lifted her head. She noticed that her father held a package. Between sniffs she asked, "Wh— what is it, D—Daddy? Wh—who sent it?"

Mr. Stevens began to open the package.

"It is from Tia Carmencita Estevan," he answered.

Carmen flopped down on her pillow with a furious snort.

"Very well," said Daddy, and started to do up the package again.

Carmen thought fast. Perhaps it would be best to see what Tia had sent. It might be her only present.

"Open it, Daddy—please," she said softly.

Daddy opened it. Carmen gasped.

"Oh, my!" she cried. "It must be a cow!"

Daddy had pulled out an object with hair all over it. It was dirty white and smelled of hide. It was a book with a jacket made of cow-hide.

Mr. Stevens began to read a letter which had come with the book. The letter was written in Spanish so Carmen could not understand it. When Mr. Stevens finished reading it he turned to her.

"Tia Carmencita has sent you this old ac-

"THIS BOOK TELLS THE STORY"

count book," he said. "It belonged to her father and a great mystery surrounds it."

He turned the pages and smiled.

"In this old book," he continued, "Tia has written her story for you, Carmen. Years ago she travelled the same road that you are going to travel on your way to Seattle. She thought you might like to take her with you on your trip."

Carmen's eyes asked a question. Mr. Stevens answered it.

"She means," he said, "that you are to read about her on your trip. How would it feel to have a little girl of long ago as a travelling companion?"

"Oh, it would be fun!" cried Carmen.

Imagine! To journey along the same road and find out what happened to a child of long ago! To have that child as a travelling companion—even if she did happen to live between the pages of a funny cow-book!

Mr. Stevens noticed the changed expression on Carmen's face. Carmen never could stay angry long. Her temper was a guest who made only very short visits.

"You see," her father said, "when Tia was a little girl, she, too, had to leave California. She, too, lost her home—her beautiful rancho."

"Why?" inquired Carmen. "Did her father sell it?"

"No," answered Mr. Stevens. "The Americans came and took it away from him."

"But how could they do that?" asked Carmen. "Wasn't it against the law?"

Mr. Stevens tapped the cow-book. "This book tells the story," he said. "And it is a mystery story."

Carmen was growing more and more interested. "Will you read it to me, Daddy?" she asked.

"Yes," he replied. "But not until you have dressed and had breakfast. Then I will read a chapter."

And because we, too, might like to hear a chapter of Tia Carmencita's cow-book story, let us make believe that it is after breakfast now.

Carmen and her father sit in their living room. Mr. Stevens takes up the cow-book.

He also has a small Spanish dictionary beside him.

"This is because my Spanish is rusty," he says.

"How can your Spanish be rusty?" asks Carmen. "Was it left out in the rain like my bicycle?"

"Well, not exactly," laughs Mr. Stevens. "But I have not used it for some time. So, in order to translate the cow-book into English for you, I must keep Mrs. Dictionary handy."

"I shall look up the words for you," said Carmen.

So Mr. Stevens began to read Carmencita's cow-book story.

CHAPTER II

CARMENCITA—YESTERDAY

THIS IS CARMENCITA'S COW-BOOK STORY

The year 1850 was to be a very important one for me. First, it was during this year that my pet pig died! Then, our state, California, was admitted to the Union. And last, our beautiful rancho was taken from us. This is how it happened:

One summer day we were having a picnic in the glen. A picnic was a great treat to Californians. The food and the girls were always so beautiful!

Great oaks spread above us. Delicious eatables spread below. Roast chickens. Tamales. Cheeses. Tortillas. Rich chocolate. Um-m! I sat beside Hipolito and our mouths watered.

21

Hipolito Estevan and his brother, Juan, were my best friends. We played together every day.

Our fathers were best friends, too, but they were too old to play. They worked together on my father's rancho. We had given the Estevans a home here ever since they had lost their own rancho.

The boys had no mother. Neither had I. Hipolito was fifteen, tall and dark, very quiet and dreamy.

Juan was twelve, short and noisy, very, very wild and always in mischief. Often he made me anxious. I was very anxious about him today, for he had not yet arrived at the picnic.

That was not like Juan, who could always eat more than anyone else and sing more loudly. Often the grown-ups lifted him on to the table and made him sing for them. They liked his boyish voice and his roguish smile.

CARMENCITA, HIPOLITO, AND JUAN

*Juan had a dimple in his cheek which he
detested. Once he had tried to stretch it
away by keeping a small apple in his cheek
for days.*

But I think that only made it worse and made him look as if he had the mumps.

Oh, Juan was a terrible boy, but still I worried about him.

"Where can he be?" I asked Hipolito.

Hipolito was swaying to the music of a guitar. "Come, dance with me, Carmencita," he said.

"No," I answered, shortly. I was cross with Hipolito. Suppose something had happened to Juan?

But just then came a crackling of branches, the hoof beats of a pony, and my heart beat faster.

With a sudden whirl, Juan's pony was there beside us with Juan on his back. The younger brother's dark eyes danced. He leaned down from his saddle close to Hipolito and me, and whispered excitedly:

"Come to the house quickly! The Yankees are there!"

"The Yankees?" I gasped. "What do

they want?   What are they doing there?"

"They are talking to your father," Juan answered me.   "I am afraid there is some trouble.   Hurry!   Let us go to the window and listen."

The Yankees had made much trouble for California land owners.   It was they who had taken the Estevans' rancho because Mr. Estevan could not prove that it belonged to him.   The Yankees wanted to see papers before they would believe.

What if they were going to take my father's rancho?   But no!   My father would never allow that.   He could prove that it was his.   He must have a paper.   He must!

Swiftly, Hipolito and I climbed up behind Juan on his pony.   Like the wind we galloped toward the house.

We stopped the pony beneath the drawing room window.   Hipolito was tall enough to look into the room.   But Juan and I had to stand up on the pony's back so we could see.

Juan kept getting in front of me and bobbing about. But I could see that my father stood in the center of our large drawing room. A group of Yankees surrounded him.

We heard one Yankee say, "Tomorrow, in the Pueblo (town) of Los Angeles, there will be a meeting of rancho owners. All who cannot show a grant to their land will lose it."

A grant was a paper proving one's rights to his rancho.

I saw my father smile and stroke his silvery mustache. I was very proud of my father in his handsome velvet suit with gold embroidery.

"Si, si (yes, yes)," he answered. "I understand. But I shall not lose my rancho, good Americanos."

The Yankees looked surprised. My father went on talking.

"Not often," he said, "must a California gentleman show pieces of paper, for his

word is enough.   But if Mister Americano wishes a paper, then I shall fetch the grant to my land."

My heart gave a joyous leap.   We did have a grant!

But I noticed that one of the men in the room scowled.   He was a tall, blond fellow who stood beside the long table.   The thought came to me that, perhaps, he wanted my father to lose his rancho.

The Yankees often made money by selling the land which they took from the Californians.   I did not like this man.

My father talked on: "The Spanish King granted this land to my people," he said.   "I keep the grant quite safe.   It is in that hide-covered account book, there on the long table."

He pointed to the old cow-book, which I had always seen in the self-same place.   In it my father sometimes wrote figures which had to do with the business of the rancho.

I FELT A LITTLE SCREAM COME OUT OF ME

So that was where he kept his grant! I was so happy to think that it was safe. And so was Juan, for quite suddenly he gave a quick jerk, which frightened the pony.

The next thing I knew something terrible had happened. Juan had fallen, head first, through the window and lay sprawling inside the drawing room.

Immediately there was great excitement. My father and several Yankees rushed to Juan's side. I was so frightened. I felt a little scream come out of me. But then I saw Juan's smile and I knew he was not hurt.

"Young rascal!" scolded my father. But there was a twinkle in his eye. "Listening at the window, eh?" He rumpled Juan's hair. "Run away now and play; we are busy."

Juan came out to Hipolito and me. He was flushed but not at all ashamed of himself. He hopped right up upon the pony's back again and we continued to watch the scene in the room as though nothing had happened.

But what happened next was the worst of all. Every time I think of it I feel like crying.

My father walked over to the table saying, "Now I shall get my grant and show it to you, gentlemen."

He opened the cow-book. He searched through its pages. The smile left his lips. A deep frown appeared between his eyes. Nobody spoke. All waited anxiously. I heard something pounding in my head, "Tung! Tung! Tung! Where is the grant? Where is the grant?"

At last my father turnea to the crowd. "It is gone!" he said.

I hardly remember what happened after that. I do know, however, that Juan behaved like a mad-man. He growled and sputtered. He even said a bad word, and jumped up and down, trampling a flower bed.

My eyes were blinded with tears and my heart ached for my poor father. Even easy-going Hipolito clenched his fists and looked fierce.

All day long the house was searched, but the grant was not found. For days I recall my father's sad eyes and worried frown.

Often I thought about that tall, blond Yankee who had stood near the long table. He could so easily have taken the grant. He could have taken it while everyone was so concerned about Juan.

Did he do it? How could a little girl nine years old know?

What I did know, however, was that we had lost our beloved rancho. Yes, my father came home from the meeting in Los Angeles a few days later and told us the news.

That night he and Mr. Estevan talked for hours. The next morning I was called into the drawing room.

There sat my father looking old, old. There sat Mr. Estevan beside him, twirling his large sombrero (Mexican hat) in his hands. There stood Hipolito and Juan with serious faces. Yes, even Juan was serious.

"You may sit down, my child," said my father.

A child of old California was never al-

lowed to sit in the presence of his elders unless first given permission. I now sat upon the arm of my father's chair.

"My children," he said. "You know that this beautiful rancho has been taken from us. I cannot prove that it belongs to me for my land grant is lost. So we are all obliged to move away."

"Where are we going, father?" I asked.

He stroked my hand. "Far in the north people are digging for gold," he replied. "Mr. Estevan and I have decided to become miners. We are going to the gold mines."

An explosion! We turned, startled. Juan was standing upon his head, letting out one war-whoop after the other.

Now, old California fathers were very strict. But, somehow, neither Mr. Estevan nor my father scolded Juan. I saw little wrinkles of amusement around both their mouths.

"Are you very glad to go to the gold coun-

THE RANCHO

try, my son?" asked Mr. Estevan. "Is that why you turn yourself upside down?"

"Si! Si! Si!" cried Juan. He jumped to his feet. His cheeks were red and the dimple showed plainly. "I shall be a miner! I shall find great gold nuggets the size of a house!" he shouted.

Then my father picked up from the long

table his hide-covered account book. He handed it to me. There was a queer, sad smile on his lips.

"Take this, my daughter," he said. "I shall need it no longer. Keep it with you on our trip and write your adventures in it. You are sure to have many on such a long and difficult journey."

My father knew how dearly I loved to scribble. I took the cow-book and thanked him.

"We leave in a week," he continued. "We go first to San Francisco, a great distance of five hundred miles. We must all be prepared to face dangers—even my little girl."

He squeezed my hand. I squeezed back some tears that tried to come out of my eyes.

"I am not afraid, Father," I said.

CHAPTER III

CITY OF ANGELS—TODAY

Mr. Stevens stopped reading, put down the old cow-book and turned to Carmen.

"And now," he said. "How would you like to drive out to see that rancho?"

Carmen's face lit up. That would be fun. Oh, she was going to have a nice birthday after all!

"Shall I see the glen where Carmencita and Hipolito went for the picnic?" she asked. "And the window that Juan fell through? Oh, I liked Juan!"

"Come along, then," said Mr. Stevens. "And tonight, if you like, we shall read some more about them."

He put the cow-book on the table.

And here is a secret—a very important

secret which nobody knows but me, because I am writing the story.

The only other person who did know it is now dead. That other person was the tall, blond Yankee who stood beside the table that day so long ago.

You remember the man who, Carmencita thought, might have stolen the grant out of the cow-book? Well, he really had stolen it! He had taken it while everyone was so startled by Juan's fall.

But after he had taken it he did not know what to do with it. First he thought he might stuff it into his pocket. Then he feared that someone might find it there and he would be arrested.

He must act quickly, for soon the excitement over Juan would be over and, the old gentleman would look for his grant.

An idea struck the tall Yankee. He noticed that the jacket of the cow-book was a bit loose. He saw a slit which made a tiny

OLVERA STREET, LOS ANGELES

opening between the thick hide covering and the book itself.

Carefully he slipped the precious grant inside this opening and pressed down the hide binding. He then sighed with relief. Nobody would ever think of looking for it there!

And nobody ever did! For, through all

the years, that grant to the rancho remained right where he put it. There it lay, flattened between the thick hide jacket and the wooden cover of the cow-book.

Even now, it was still there, right in Carmen Stevens' living room! Oh, Carmen, if you only knew that! But it is our secret.

Now, back to Carmen and her father. They drove off in the Ford. Carmen did not like to ride in that cheap little car. She hoped nobody would see her. Especially Betty-next-door, who owned a large car.

"On our way to the rancho," said her father, "we shall explore our city. It may be many years before we return to it."

As they drove, he told her that Los Angeles is the largest city in area in the United States. The Spanish name is "La Reina de Los Angeles"—"Queen of the Angels."

"We are now on Figueroa Street," said Mr. Stevens. "It was named after the Governor of California. But, like other Los Angeles streets, it was not always called that.

"Once it was known as Street of the Grasshoppers because from the wild lands all about, grasshoppers came down into the heart of the town.

"Some of the finest homes were built on Grasshopper Street after the pests were gone. But imagine how you would feel if you had to admit that you lived on Grasshopper Street.   So the name was changed.

"Castelar Street once was Bull Street because the Spanish, you know, were very fond of bull fights.

"When Tia Carmencita lived in Los Angeles," Mr. Stevens went on, "there were no automobiles. Spanish caballeros, cow-boys and Indians rode about on horseback.

"Often there were lawless shootings and Indian battles. Wild animals came down from the hills."

He pointed to the modern streets and tall buildings, the many automobiles.

"Now the only wild beasts we have to fear are those motor cars," he said. "Los Angeles has changed—oh, a little bit. Eh, Carmen mio?"

Carmen knew that "mio" meant "my" in Spanish. She loved to hear her father speak the language of old California. With his white teeth and brown skin, he reminded her of pictures of Spanish noblemen. She was proud of him just as Carmencita had been proud of her father.

"But now, Señorita (miss)," he continued, "we shall stop at a place which has not changed at all. Olvera Street is the oldest street in Los Angeles. It has been kept just as it used to be in the long ago."

Together they stepped out of the Ford and into the past. They walked down a cobbled street filled with gay, Mexican booths. Everyone was making something, selling something or singing something. It was like a bit of old Mexico.

A woman was cooking Mexican pancakes right on the street. Carmen's father stopped and bought her one.

"Ugh!" she coughed. "It tastes like cardboard!"

"My ancestors were brought up on these tortillas," said her father. "They did not turn into hat boxes!"

They visited the old Avila House.

"This was the home of Doña Avila, a Spanish lady," said Mr. Stevens. "In 1846 she gave many fine horses from her rancho to help in the war. It was the time when the last battles were being fought between the Americans and the native Californians."

"What was Tia Carmencita doing at that time?" asked Carmen.

Suddenly, the old aunt had become very interesting to her. It must have been the cow-book story waiting for her at home.

"She was just a little girl then," said Mr. Stevens. "She lived out on the rancho, and that is where we are going now."

AN ICE-CREAM PARLOR NEAR LOS ANGELES

On the way they passed ice-cream parlors and shops built in the shapes of cream jugs, mushrooms, even huge dolls; gas stations that looked like Oriental palaces, blue houses without windows and some that belonged inside the pages of fairy books.

"What do you think is the most interest-

THE HOLLYWOOD BOWL

ing thing in Los Angeles today, Daddy?" asked Carmen.

"I would say," replied her father, "the old Spanish landmarks, or Hollywood Bowl where symphonies under the stars are given every summer. Or, La Brea Oil Pits where great beasts roamed years ago and were later found buried in the oil."

"But," he continued, "do you know what people will first ask you about when you move to another state?"

LA BREA OIL PITS

Carmen could not imagine what it could be. "Tell me, Daddy," she said.

"The movies," answered her father. "Hollywood is the center of picture making and

everyone is interested in how the movies are
made. Look!"

Mr. Stevens slowed the car and pointed to
a group of people, trucks and cameras on
the side of the road.

"Here is a movie company now and we can
watch them working," he said.

Carmen saw the company of actors making a scene from a comedy. While the
cameras ground, a battered automobile,
driven by a yellow-faced funny man,
crashed right into a small barn and de-
stroyed it. The man drove out, grinning
and unhurt.

"How could he do that, Daddy?" asked
Carmen. "Was he a magician?"

They had left the scene and were driving
on their way once more.

Mr. Stevens answered by asking a question. "Do you see that tall, white flower
growing on the hill over there?" he asked.

"Yes," said Carmen. "It is a yucca. But

why didn't you answer me about the funny man who crashed through the barn?"

"I did answer," smiled her father. "The reason the movie folk can crash into barns and not get hurt is because of that yucca plant. You see, when they wish to break things, they make them out of the soft pith of the yucca stalks.

"The yucca flowers are called 'God's Candles' because they are so straight and beautiful. It takes about twenty years for them to bloom."

At the old Mission of San Gabriel they stopped. Black-robed priests and little Mexican children were praying in the chapel. The odor of incense filled the cool halls. In the court Carmen saw small models of all the Missions, for there are twenty-one in California.

"We shall see most of these on our way north," said Mr. Stevens. "Each one has its own story."

YUCCAS—"GOD'S CANDLES"

"Tell me the story of this one, Daddy," said Carmen.

After they had climbed to the bell tower, they settled themselves comfortably in the court and Mr. Stevens told Carmen the

story. It is called "The Bells of San
Gabriel." Here it is:

Don Rafael, a young Spanish soldier,
sailed to California with the priests. In
Spain, Augustina, his dearly beloved, waited
for him to return. They were going to be
married.

But one day an arrow pierced the heart of
Don Rafael. Poor Augustina! When she
heard of his death, there lived no sadder
lady in all Spain.

One day, the Spaniards were to cast the
bells for the young mission, San Gabriel, far
away in California. Liquid metal was to be
poured into great molds to shape the bells.

A crowd gathered in the Spanish town.
Augustina stood among the people. She
knew that these bells were soon to be sent
to California, to the spot where Don Rafael
slept.

Augustina wore a gold cross and a ring
which her lover had given her. The sorrow-

ing maiden said a prayer as she bent over the furnace. Then she dropped her golden cross and ring into the boiling mass of metal.

When the crowd saw this, a strange thing happened to them. They, too, began to pray and to throw their ornaments and jewels into the boiling pot.

Some say that the love and faith of these people have given the bells of San Gabriel their golden voice.

"What happened to Augustina, Daddy?" asked Carmen.

"A very odd thing," answered Mr. Stevens. "But when I tell you, remember that this is only a legend.

"One evening, as Augustina sat alone in chapel, a beautiful smile came over her face. She murmured, 'The bells are ringing and my Rafael hears.' Then she passed away.

"Later, the people of Spain learned that

SAN GABRIEL MISSION

on the day of Augustina's death, the bells of
San Gabriel had first rung out in California."

Carmen and her father visited the largest
grapevine in the world. It covers 10,000
square feet, is nine feet around, and has
lived for more than one hundred years.

It grows in the garden of Ramona's home.
Ramona was the heroine of a famous book
by Helen Hunt Jackson, about the Mission
Indians of California. It has been called
the Indian "Uncle Tom's Cabin."

Carmen felt a thrill as they neared Carmencita's old rancho home. Lazy oak trees,
bent with age, sprawled over the ground. A
mist of heat caressed the brown mountains.

The house was made of adobe, or sun-
baked mud. It looked peaceful and settled.
Like some old, squat Spanish woman to
whom time means but little.

Porches, like ample bosoms, encircled the
house. The air about was soft, like the ac-

cents of the people who once dwelt there. The hills sent down a perfume of sage brush.

"Oh, Daddy!" cried Carmen. "If only we could live here instead of in Seattle with that old . . ."

She was going to say "that old Tia," but she stopped herself. Why, "that old Tia" was little Carmencita whom she liked so much.

"The unfortunate part is," said Mr. Stevens, "that this rancho still belongs to Tia. That is, if someone could really prove that the grant did exist."

"I am sure it did," said Carmen, firmly. "Carmencita's father had it from the King of Spain. What is a grant, Daddy?"

Mr. Stevens explained, "A grant is a writing on paper, telling that certain land belongs to a certain person. It is usually given by a public office. In Spanish they would call the papers 'expediente'."

RAMONA'S MARRIAGE PLACE

"Well, I know that horrid Yankee took the grant when no one was looking. I know he did!" said Carmen.

Thoughtfully she stroked the soft hide of the cow-book.

"And, just think," she added, "He took it out of this very book!"

But Carmen did not know that the Yankee had also put it back into that very book! Inside the jacket of the very book she now held!

"Will you read to me this evening about Carmencita, Daddy?" she asked.

"Yes," promised Mr. Stevens. "And every evening on our trip. In that way, you shall follow Carmencita's trip, too."

"Shall we travel the same road?" asked Carmen.

"Almost the same," answered Mr. Stevens. "But our journey will be much shorter. Things have greatly changed since that day. Airplanes now fly to San Francisco from Los Angeles in a few hours. The next cow-book chapter will tell you what that same journey meant to Carmencita in the year 1850."

CHAPTER IV

BANDITS!—YESTERDAY

This Is Carmencita's Cow-Book Story

We were going to leave the rancho. Yes, tomorrow! All was packed and in readiness.

We were to ride in a stage coach all the way to San Francisco! What a long and dangerous journey!

I had heard of Indians, wild animals, bandits along the road. But that did not bother me so much as the thought of leaving my dear rancho.

Everyone went around with sad faces. Even the servants cried. Yes, even fat, growly cook.

Now I lay in bed and cried, too. Then I

stopped crying for I heard someone singing under my window.

Often young men would serenade young ladies at night.   But I was only a little girl, so young men did not sing to me.   Who could it be?

Then I recognized that voice!   Juan's. He had been so excited all day that he had nearly driven us all frantic.   He had made himself a funny banjo out of the bottom of a pan.   He had strung wire across it.   It made a dreadful sound.

"Tang!   Tung!   Bum!" went the "pan-jo."   Juan's voice grew louder.   He had learned a song that the gold miners sing:

> *"Oh, California!*
>   *That's the land for me,*
>   *I'm going to Sacramento,*
>   *With my wash bowl on my knee!"*

A window opened on the floor below me. I heard a splash and a squeal.   I jumped out of bed and ran to my window. I saw Juan dripping with water, running off as fast as he could. Cook's head drew in from the window below.

I went back to bed and wished that I could be as excited and happy as Juan.

Next day we left for San Francisco. The regular stage coach line from Los Angeles to San Francisco did not start running until several years later. So we had to go in a covered wagon with a party of other gold seekers.

Many people were going North now. Everyone had heard that tempting call— "Gold!" Some had become very rich at the mines. They had found large golden nuggets in the ground. The largest ever found weighed one hundred and ninety-five pounds. That is about the weight of your father—if he is fat!

From San Francisco we were to go to Sacramento and then up into the mountains.

Here our fathers were to dig for the precious metal.

We left Los Angeles early in the morning. The wagon jolted and bumped. I had to hold on hard.

I heard some of the men in the wagon talking together. "It was right here," said one, "that a party was held up by robbers two months ago."

Juan's eyes sparkled. He clutched his precious gun. Nobody could take that gun away from him. He even slept with it. And it was a beautiful gun. But it had one fault. It would not shoot! Still, Juan was happy with it.

We passed prairie schooners, people on horseback and on foot. Once I saw a carreta (a rough wooden-wheeled cart) full of laughing girls. They were going to a picnic.

They looked so pretty in their shawls, with tall combs in their hair. One played a guitar. It made me very sad for I thought

"I'LL PROTECT YOU," JUAN SAID

of the happy days we were leaving behind us.

The men in our wagon began to talk of bears in the mountains. "Those big grizzlies can whip the strongest African lion," they said.

I gripped my father's hand. Tomorrow

we should be in the mountains. I wanted my father near me all the time. When he was out of my sight I felt afraid.

Juan would puff out his chest and say, "I will protect you!" He would shoulder his gun and make a fierce face. But still I was afraid.

Hipolito said very little. I know he thought much about our lovely, lazy rancho. Hipolito did not fancy the idea of being a miner.

We stopped the first night in a small, ugly town. There was a tavern here where we had our dinner. The food was very bad but we were hungry, so we ate it.

Our rooms had no windows, but a door led into the patio, or garden. A great bar of wood fastened the door. Why? Indians? Bears?

The bed was hard. The blankets were not clean. But in spite of all this, I was so tired that I soon fell asleep.

Next day we reached the mountains. We were becoming accustomed to our swaying wagon. We were quite happy. But, oh, we were hungry!

It was toward dusk and Juan and I were amusing ourselves. Do you know what we were doing? We were talking about food!

"I shall have for supper dark red chile peppers, hot, hot, hot!" said Juan. "Ah, and then a sauce of olive oil with crushed tomatoes and garlic. Over this, chopped onions and cheese!"

I could almost taste it. Umm! How good!

"And I shall have—" I began.

But I got no further, for, just then, from behind us came a noise of thunder! We turned. Galloping horsemen, with knives and guns, were shouting at us to stop. Bandits!

Our wagon stopped so suddenly that I was nearly thrown out. The noisy robbers circled about us. Our women grew white and all of the men's eyes flashed with anger.

But everyone stepped out and we held our hands above our heads while the robbers took everything away from us—even my little gold chain left to me by my mother.

Then they galloped away as suddenly as they had come.

We started off again.   After we had been on our way for several minutes, I missed Juan.

"Father!" I cried. "Juan is gone!"

We looked. No Juan.

"Stop the wagon!" cried my father.

But just then we heard a noise from the rear of the wagon where we kept the luggage. Huddled among the bags and boxes we found Juan. He was bound and gagged. He clutched something in his hand. We unbound him and he told us his story.

"While the bandits had us lined up across the stream," he said, "I was watching one of them as he climbed into our wagon.   I

BRAVE LITTLE JUAN!

ducked down under Mr. Loomis' large stomach and nobody saw me sneak over to the wagon.

"The bandit was stealing from our lug-

gage, and I saw him taking Carmencita's cow-book. I know how much Carmencita loves that book, so I pointed my gun at the bandit and he dropped it quickly.

"I snatched it up, but the bandit seized me and threw me down. He tied me up and went on stealing.

"But he forgot about the cow-book, and, see, Carmencita, I have saved it for you!"

Perhaps I should never have written this story if it had not been for Juan. Brave little Juan with his gun that did not shoot!

CHAPTER V

THE GOLDEN COAST—TODAY

Several days later the Stevens family was ready to leave on their modern journey. Mother's pillows and blankets and medicines were already packed in the auto. The suitcases had a nice neat home on a shelf in back of the car.

Carmen gave a last look at her house. Tears filled her eyes and her throat swelled.

Then she gazed up at a window next door and there was Betty, her neighbor. Betty, watching her, with a proud, silly smile on her face. Smiling at Carmen who had to move away in a cheap little car! Stupid, horrid girl!

Carmen flounced into the car beside her father, her nose in the air. She wouldn't let Betty see that her heart was breaking.

They were off—starting their trip along the Golden Coast! Carmen recalled Carmencita of old jogging in her rattly coach.

"Daddy," asked Carmen, "is this the same road that Tia Carmencita travelled last night?"

Mr. Stevens started in amazement. "Last night?" he asked.

Carmen laughed. "Oh, I meant in the chapter you read to me last night," she explained.

"Yes, it is the same road," answered her father. "But so different!"

Carmen did not have to be told that. Smooth highways, speeding motor cars, gasoline stations, comfortable hotels.

No bears. No Indians. A peaceful, civilized land.

How grateful she should be in her soft-cushioned, rubber-tired automobile. Betty-next-door might sniff at it because it was a cheap little car. But Carmencita of old would have thought it a fairy coach.

Each part of the country seemed so different. There were stretches of golden beach, orange groves, miles of huge oak trees, peaceful farms, and a district of pink beans.

They were on El Camino Real, "The King's Highway." Once this road was like a chain that strung together the old Missions.

The Spanish padres, or priests, built these Missions almost two hundred years ago. They built them all the way from San Diego to far North.

Let us go back to olden times and listen to the ringing of the Mission bells calling the Indians to prayer. These Indians were very poor and dirty.

But look! Now the padres are setting up a cross. Here comes Father Junipero Serra, the saintly priest who is head of the Missions.

In his beautiful, kind eyes is a glow of joy, for today he is going to baptize the first Indian child. He will sprinkle it with holy water. An Indian mother has at last agreed to bring her baby to the Mission.

But see the frightened look in the brown mother's eyes. She loves the good padre; still she is afraid.

Father Serra gently takes the little papoose and starts to sprinkle water upon its head. But suddenly the Indian mother snatches her child and runs away.

This is a sad day for Father Serra. He will always wonder whether he was to blame because that baby's soul was lost.

Yet it was not long before many Indians came to the Mission to be baptized and did not run away. They came and stayed, and lived and worked there.

Mission life was full of beauty and color. See the women spinning and the men tilling the soil. Do you hear those Indian children droning over their school lessons? And beneath the olive trees sit a group of boys playing upon musical instruments.

But the padres are very strict, not only with their pupils but with themselves. Let us go toward the garden where tall palms are waving and a fountain is playing.

Let us listen to what the head padre is saying to some young student priests.

"Take off those shoes and stockings, brothers," he says. "Thou must learn to wear only sandals upon thy feet."

Then he points to a blazing fire in the distance.

"Today we are burning all the carts in the Mission," he says. "We must go about our work on foot."

The story is told of Father Serra walking for many miles though suffering from an injured leg. When the pain grew so terrible that he could bear it no longer, he called to one of his mule-drivers.

Courtesy of San Diego Chamber of Commerce
SAN DIEGO DE ALCALA, FIRST CALIFORNIA MISSION

"Boy," he said. "Hast thou no remedy for my sore leg?"

The mule-driver replied, "I have but

remedies for beasts, father—not for men."

"Then treat me like a beast," said the padre, "and cure me as if I were thy mule."

The boy mixed some herbs in hot tallow and rubbed them on the wound. Next morning Father Serra's leg was better.

But this sore never quite healed and always caused him great suffering. Still, to the end of his life, he would walk barefoot from one Mission to the other, a distance of many weary miles.

The first Mission was founded near San Diego, which is at the very toe of California. It was in San Diego that Charles Lindbergh's monoplane, "The Spirit of St. Louis," was built.

San Diego's harbor is the headquarters for the Eleventh U. S. Naval District, and on Point Loma is the oldest and highest lighthouse on the Pacific Coast.

Old Town, which is now part of San Diego, is where the first palm tree was planted and also where the American flag was first raised in California! A city of "first" and important happenings!

"All the way up the Coast we find people of different nations," said Mr. Stevens. "Six flags have waved over California and each one has left some souvenir behind."

"I know two," said Carmen. "The Spanish and American flags."

"Those were the first and last," said her father. "In between came the English, the Russian, the Mexican and the Bear Flag of the State."

That evening they dined at a hotel set in the midst of a flower garden.

"We could have reached San Francisco tonight," said Mr. Stevens. "But we shall stop here so mother can rest."

"Will you read another chapter from the cow-book, Daddy?" asked Carmen.

"First you must go to your room and unpack your suitcase," replied her father.

"Oh, what a bother!" exclaimed Carmen. "I wish Minnie were here to do it for me!"

Minnie was her maid.

"There will be no more Minnies for you, young lady," said Mr. Stevens. "You must learn to do things for yourself. Now, hurry, or I shall not read to you."

Carmen sighed. The scowl on her forehead became very busy. But she wanted to hear more about Carmencita, so she went to her hotel bedroom.

What a sweet little room it was! Clean and white, with flowered curtains at the windows.

She started to unpack. Such a nuisance to unpack things and then pack them up again in the morning! On other trips Minnie had been along to do that for her. When Betty-next-door went travelling she always had her maid to help her.

Angry tears stung Carmen's eyes. She pulled nightclothes and toilet articles out of her suitcase and flung them all over the bed in a rage.

Then, suddenly, she began to think of Carmencita. Poor Carmencita of old in that ugly tavern! No windows. A hard bed with blankets that were not even clean. Bars on the windows to keep out Indians and bears.

She looked out of her window and saw a Mexican gardener, whistling at his work. A friendly dog was sniffing at the flower beds. Everything was so safe for Carmen of today; everyone so friendly.

The scowl disappeared. She picked up her things and put them away.

She went into her parents' room. Mother was complaining. The lights were not bright enough. The water was not hot enough. Her head ached so. The trip had been tiring! Poor Mother!

But Carmen could not help wondering what her mother would have said had she been obliged to travel in that wagon of old!

MR. STEVENS READ TO CARMEN

"Come along now, chick," said Father.
"Kiss Mother good night and then for a
chapter of the cow book. You may go and
fetch it out of my suitcase."

Before handing the cow-book to her father, Carmen looked at it intently. How much that little book could tell!

Mr. Stevens seemed to read her thoughts. "It has lived a long time and holds a great deal!" he said.

But Mr. Stevens did not know how true his words really were. He was only thinking of the story which the cow-book held. We know, however, that it held more than just a story!

It held that important grant—the grant to the rancho!

Here is the chapter that Mr. Stevens read to Carmen that night.

CHAPTER VI

FIRE!—YESTERDAY

THIS IS CARMENCITA'S COW-BOOK STORY

After what seemed like years, we reached San Francisco! Of course it was not years. It was really only days, but there were many, many of them, full of bumps and jolts, frights and discomfort!

How happy we were to arrive in a town once more!

Perhaps no stranger town ever existed than San Francisco in 1850. All over the many hills were small tents and funny looking mushroom huts.

It appeared as if Mr. and Mrs. Everybody, their children and dogs had come to San Francisco! Father told me that they were here for the same reason that we were. Gold!

Soon we should be joining the streams of people on their way to Sacramento. Then Father and Mr. Estevan would start to be miners. But we must stay in San Francisco a few days first while the two men arranged their business affairs.

How I enjoyed that city! Only a few years ago San Francisco had been called Yerba Buena, which means "good herb," because a mint-like vine grew along the shores.

The name was difficult to spell and to pronounce, so it was changed to San Francisco, after the well-known bay.

Some say that San Francisco Bay had its name from St. Francis of Assisi, founder of the religious order of Franciscan Fathers who started the Missions. But perhaps it was named after Sir Francis Drake, the first man to touch these shores.

Yerba Buena was just a quiet little Span-

SAN FRANCISCO BAY

ish town. Then came the "gold rush" and many people left for the mines. San Francisco went to sleep.

But one day a wonderful thing happened. Through the Golden Gate came the first steamer from the East. Flags waved, bands played, everyone cheered. That was the be-

ginning of San Francisco's great awakening.

Though many still went to the mines, others also came back to the City of Hills, to spend the gold they had dug.

Juan and Hipolito and I walked around the streets. Everyone seemed so busy and rich. Everything cost so very much. Big, noisy miners stalked about or drove beautiful teams of horses.

We stopped beside a fruit stand. Juan wanted to buy oranges. He asked for six. The fruit vender smiled.

"Six dollars," he said.

Juan nearly fell head-first into the fruit cart. He jingled fifty cents in his pocket. It was all he had.

"Then, just for that," he returned, "I don't want any!"

At that moment a great, tall miner stopped. He looked at us in a curious way. I drew closer to Hipolito and Juan.

"A dozen oranges! A dozen pears! A

dozen apples!" bellowed the miner to the fruit vender.

He did not take his eyes off of us. The vender gave him his fruit and we saw him throw fifty dollars in gold over the counter.

Then he came close to me and put his hand on my head. He smiled and said, "I have a little girl, too. I have not seen her for a long time. She is in Missouri."

When the vender gave him his change, he put it into my hand. "Buy yourself something," he said, and departed.

We explored the city. The streets were in a frightful condition. We laughed as we read this funny sign: "THIS STREET IS IMPASSABLE. NOT EVEN JACKASS-ABLE."

Covered wagons lined the water front. In them, brave people had journeyed across the plains with the cry, "California or bust!" Now they were living in those wagons.

Ships in the harbor. Oh, how many

ships! Some were being used as stores, hotels, houses, because they would never sail the seas again.

When we grew tired of roaming the city, we started for our hotel. An unpleasant surprise greeted us! My father and Mr. Estevan had something important to say. They looked very grave.

"My dear little daughter," said Father, drawing me close to him, "We are leaving for the gold mines tomorrow."

I could see nothing sad in this.

But then Mr. Estevan threw his arm about Juan's shoulder and said, "You, Juan, must promise to be a good boy and take care of Carmencita while we are gone."

"What—what do you mean, Father?" I cried. I was beginning to understand. Juan and I were not going to the mines!

"Tomorrow morning a kind lady is coming to fetch you and Juan," said my father. "You will board and lodge with her and go to school here in San Francisco. A mine is no place for children."

I heard Juan gasp. Left behind! Not permitted to go to the mines!

The scene that followed was not a credit to Juan and me! We disgraced ourselves and I was just as naughty as Juan.

But all we got for our trouble was to be sent to bed without supper. However, Hipolito managed to sneak us some bread. But Juan, bad boy, threw it in his face.

That is how furious Juan was. I think he must have torn his bed clothes to shreds and kicked the slats out of his bed! Poor Juan! How he had counted upon being a miner!

I lay awake a long time in misery. My dear father was leaving me! It was the cruelest thing that had ever happened to me in all my life!

Then, before I knew it I must have fallen asleep, for suddenly I was awake again.

What was that strange smell? I sat up

in bed and saw a terrible sight. Clouds of grey smoke were coming through my window. Outside I saw leaping flames.

I heard hurried footsteps in the hall, and a woman's voice screaming, "The city's a-fire again!"

My father rushed into my room, lifted me into his arms and carried me out.

From all sides I heard, "The city's on fire!"

We fled. Soon we were on a hilltop. People all around us were making their beds upon the ground. Someone gave my father a blanket and he covered me up.

"Go to sleep, little one," he said. "We are safe now."

But I could not sleep. I looked down from the hill upon the burning town. People were rushing about the streets trying to save their possessions. Others were fleeing toward the hills.

"This is the second big fire since I have

lived here," said someone. "They'll have to stop building those tents and cloth houses."

It was indeed a pity that San Francisco had to burn. But since it had to, I am glad that it did on that particular night. For my father and Mr. Estevan decided not to leave Juan and me behind!

They decided to take us along to the mines! Yes, we were really going to the mines!

CHAPTER VII

GOLDEN GATE CITY—TODAY

As Carmen Stevens entered San Francisco of today she looked for the funny mushroom huts and flimsy tents. Where were the rugged miners who threw gold all about? Where were the rough streets, the covered wagons, the ships?

Carmen saw instead steep, but well-paved, hills, tall apartment houses, beautiful parks and crowded city streets.

The Stevens family settled themselves in a hotel which sat like a stone queen upon a lofty hill. The first thing that Carmen did was to unpack the precious cow-book and set it upon a table.

Today, a tour of the city, and tonight Father would read some more. Tomorrow

CHINATOWN, SAN FRANCISCO

they would start for the mountains and visit
Lake Tahoe.

"Come, my dear," said Mr. Stevens to
Carmen. "Let us take a walk through
Chinatown. I think you will enjoy that."

San Francisco's Chinatown is a famous
place. In days gone by fierce battles called

tong wars were fought here among the Chinese. Even yet an occasional outbreak occurs. But today the streets seemed peaceful enough.

Carmen and her father bought a Chinese kimono for Mother, who had stayed at home to rest. Then they stopped to examine queer-looking fish outside of a Chinese market. Odors were very busy around there.

Mr. Stevens showed Carmen the Golden Gate. It is not a gate and it is not gold. It is a beautiful harbor joining the Pacific Ocean and San Francisco Bay.

They visited the Presidio where the soldiers live. It is one of the largest military parks in the United States.

Then they went to Golden Gate Park— San Francisco's pride. Parts of this immense park are forest and parts are lake lands. Parts are flower gardens and parts are playgrounds.

Carmen rode on a merry-go-round and a

swing and a donkey, and in a goat cart. She paid a visit to the zoo and called upon kangaroo, spotted deer and antelope. She

DUTCH WINDMILL IN GOLDEN GATE PARK

wanted very much to take home a very roly-poly baby bear.

She drank tea and ate rice cakes at the quaint Japanese Tea Garden. She saw the great Dutch windmill which, her father explained, was used to pump water for the man-made lakes in the park. When it was built, it was the largest windmill in the world.

On the way home they passed a market with tempting fruit on display. Carmen thought of Juan and the fruit vender.

"If I asked for six dollars' worth of oranges, Daddy," she said, "what would happen?"

"You would almost need a truck to carry them home in," laughed Mr. Stevens.

A mild little man walked up to the Japanese clerk. "Ten cents' worth of grapes," he said.

He gave the clerk one dollar. Carmen pushed closer. With a mischievous smile, she whispered to her father, "Do you think he will give me the change?"

But when the gentleman's change came back he counted it carefully and gave Carmen only a very glassy look! Then he put the money tenderly into his pocket.

Mr. Stevens took Carmen's hand and led

STREET IN SAN FRANCISCO

her away. They could not help laughing.

"The miner gave Carmencita his change," pouted Carmen, pretending to be hurt.

"The only change you will see today, my dear," replied her father, "is the change in times!"

They walked back to their hotel. Carmen

seemed to feel motion and life all about her. Everybody walked briskly. Even street cars appeared to prance.

That evening Carmen sat by a window in their hotel and waited for her father to come and read to her. She opened the cow-book and looked at the even, flowing writing. Little Carmencita was "Tia" now—an old, very old Auntie!

Carmen caressed the jacket of the cow-book. What smooth, soft hair it had! No doubt it was made from the hide of a cow raised on their own rancho.

If only they could prove that that rancho still belonged to them! If only that lost grant could be found! And, all the time, it lay under Carmen's hand as she caressed the cow-book!

"Ready for another chapter?" asked Mr. Stevens, as he came into the room.

Carmen was quite ready, so Mr. Stevens sat down beside her and began to read.

CHAPTER VIII

GOLD!—YESTERDAY

THIS IS CARMENCITA'S COW-BOOK STORY

To Sacramento on a steamer! It sounded so nice, but it was not. It meant five days of discomfort.

We had to get off the boat each night and camp on the shore. That was, of course, fun for the boys, though it was also hard work.

One of the passengers on the steamer was a Russian with very long black whiskers. My father told me that the Russians had once tried to conquer California. Some of their fur-trading posts, long deserted, still remained.

At last we reached Sacramento, in the heart of the gold rush. It was settled by Captain John A. Sutter, and, at first, it had been called Sutter's Fort.

In 1848 a man named John Marshall was working at a saw mill near Sutter's Fort when he happened to see a small, shining object in the ground. He picked it up. It was gold!

Soon every man, woman and child knew that there was gold in California. From north, east and south came wagons, boats, pack mules, men on foot. Gold!

Came youths and grandfathers, honest folk and wicked bandits, farmers, merchants, rich and poor.

We stayed in Sacramento only long enough to make ready to leave. What a busy place! What speed and action! For quiet Spanish ranchers like ourselves it was certainly a great change.

Hipolito looked out of his dreamy eyes and continued to move in his slow, lazy way. But not Juan. Juan took on the speed and action of the North. He fairly sped!

The excitement seemed to creep into his

veins and make him wild. He darted about and plunged into everything, like a mosquito.

He went up to people on the streets and asked questions. Of course they did not understand his Spanish tongue. So Juan decided to learn their language.

Now, miners' language was peculiar. But Juan felt very proud of the few words he picked up. "Sabe," "lingo," "Injuns," "bad man," he repeated over and over. But he had no idea what he was saying.

Father and Mr. Estevan made plans and soon we were on our way to the "diggings," as the mining camps were called.

We rode in a covered wagon with a man and his wife who had come across the plains. They were very kind, but they charged my father a great sum of money to take us.

Still, everyone charged great sums for everything. We hoped that soon we would find our own great sums in the soil.

Of course, many did not "strike it rich." But we were eager and cheerful and we seemed to feel that we should be lucky.

At last we reached our "diggings." Mining camps had such funny names: "Squabbletown," "Lazy Man's Canyon," "Shinbone Peak," "Humpback Slide," "Slug Gulch," "Whiskey Diggins," "You Bet."

Ours was a sad-looking, dusty place of huts and tents. We found a little hut and rented it for a price that should have made it ashamed of itself!

It was such a discouraged-looking little hut! But, anyway, it was to be our home.

Father had arranged with the covered wagon lady to come over every day and cook for us. I was to help her take care of the house. I felt very grown-up—like a mother with four big boys.

But it was not the fun I thought it was going to be. We had no fresh vegetables nor meat. The little hut was bare and cold.

All day long my father and Mr. Estevan were away, digging for gold. I spent much time with the covered wagon lady. She taught me to cook and she even made me a doll.

But I grew tired of being with her. Hipolito and Juan always disappeared after breakfast. I fancied they went exploring and I longed to go with them. But they never invited me.

Juan grew more and more wild. His father had to scold or punish him every evening for something he had done during the day.

Once, while walking down the street, he came upon a group of Chinese. They carried long poles over their shoulders. Hanging from the poles were all sorts of peddlers' goods. Tools, boxes, baskets, bags!

Juan stopped close beside them and listened to their Chinese chatter. They were excited about something and did not notice

JUAN GREW MORE AND MORE WILD

*him.   Their shrill voices and strange words
amused him.*

*He kept silent as long as he could.   Then,
suddenly, he burst out laughing and
screamed, "Ho! Ho! No sabe lingo! Injuns! Bad man! Snakes! Hoo!"*

They turned with jerks and squeals.

Down dropped their poles. All their wares cluttered to the ground—tools, bags, boxes. —Bang!

They looked about for the "creature" which had startled them. But "it" had disappeared. "It" was gone.

So they began to pick up their wares, and under the masses of goods they found Juan! In their sudden fright, the Chinese had dropped everything on top of him.

But he was not hurt. Juan was never hurt. Yet that night he did not sit down for supper. In fact, he could not sit down comfortably for several days. That was because of Mr. Estevan and a stout stick!

Mischief like this often brought disgrace upon Juan. Most of his tricks were harmless, but one led us into serious trouble. Did I say that Juan was never hurt? I was wrong. Listen.

One morning Hipolito invited me to go out with him. He must have noticed how sad I looked when Juan left without even saying good-bye. He must have known how much I had wanted each day to go with them.

"Juan and I have found a claim," said Hipolito. "I am going there now to dig for gold. Do you want to come?"

Every man had his own claim, the place where he went to dig. It belonged to him. Nobody else had the right to touch it.

I was so happy trailing after tall Hipolito. He carried a pick over his shoulder. He led me into the hills. He seemed to know just where to go. Juan and he had been there before.

"Here it is," he said, at last. "We are certain to find gold. See."

He pointed to the soil. Sure enough, it seemed to be a slightly different color from other parts of the hill. I smiled at Hipolito. But then I noticed a large shovel lying on the ground.

Now, the miners' law said that a claim be-

longed to a man as long as he left one tool upon it. If anyone touched that claim— well, miners carried guns, and those guns were not like Juan's. They could shoot— and did!

But we had never heard of this law.

"Whose shovel is this?" I asked. "Is it yours, Hipolito?"

Hipolito shook his head. "No, it is not," he replied.

I picked up the shovel. "Do you think that this claim may belong to someone else?" I asked.

Hipolito examined the shovel. Then he threw it down.

"No matter," he said. "Whoever owned it has gone away. It belongs to us now."

Hipolito dug and dug. I helped him. There was a great deal of yellow earth and, all at once, Hipolito gave a shout. He held up a large golden rock.

"Gold!" he cried. "Really gold!"

I had never seen Hipolito so excited. I rushed over and looked at the beautiful thing. It glittered. It shone. It was gold! Oh, surely, it was gold! We were all going to be rich! What would my father say!

But just then we heard a deep growl from behind the bushes. We turned.

"What was that?" I asked Hipolito.

A deep rough voice answered me. "I am the owner of the mine," it said. "Put down that gold!"

Then we saw the point of a gun sticking through the thick bushes.

"Put up your hands," came the voice again. "You have broken the miners' law and taken my claim."

"We did not know that it belonged to you," said Hipolito stoutly.

"You should have known the law," said the voice. "You saw my shovel lying there. I am going to punish both of you. I am going to shoot!"

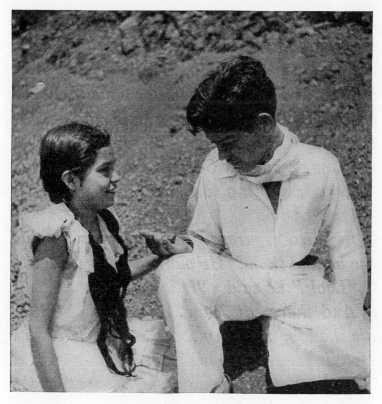

"GOLD!" HE CRIED

*I shrank back. But Hipolito rushed right
into the bushes, right into the very mouth of
that gun! I heard a terrible scuffle going on
back there. I did not know what to do.*

*Hipolito was brave but he was only a boy.
He was fighting with a big miner!*

*I must run for help. I started down the
hill, shouting. But I had not gone far when
I heard Hipolito's voice calling me back. I
turned.*

*"Come back, Carmencita," he said.
"There is nothing to fear."*

I went back.

*Hipolito separated the bushes so I could
see behind them. He pointed to an object.*

"Look," he said. "It is only Juan."

*And there sat Juan, holding his head in
his hands, swaying back and forth and
moaning. I ran to his side.*

*"What has happened? Oh, what is the
matter, Juan?" I cried.*

*Hipolito answered me. "One of his silly
pranks again," he said. "The voice talking
to us from behind the bushes was only his.
And it was his old, useless gun sticking out
at us."*

JUAN HELD HIS HEAD AND MOANED HORRIBLY

"Oh, oh, oh," groaned Juan. He rocked back and forth. He must have been in pain. I knelt down beside him. "Juan, are you hurt?" I asked, my voice trembling.

*He began to sputter, "Hip—Hippo—
ooooooo!"   He ended in a wail.*

*"When I sprang on him," said Hipolito,
"he fell and hit his head against a rock.   He
should learn not to frighten people and play
jokes like that."*

*I saw then that Juan was really badly
hurt.   There was a gash in his head.*

*"Come, Hipolito," I said.   "We must take
him home quickly."*

*We helped Juan to his feet.   He held his
head and moaned horribly.   I was so frightened.*

*But as we passed the mine where Hipolito
and I had been digging, I saw Juan smile
through his pain.   Then he gave a fierce kick
at the yellow earth.*

*"Dig up all the gold, Hipolito!" he said.
"Don't leave one beautiful rock.   They are
all painted so well.   I painted them myself!"*

*Then he gave a terrible moan.   "Oh, my
head!   My poor head!"*

CHAPTER IX

WONDERLANDS—TODAY

Back to the Stevens family in modern San Francisco.

Next day Carmen and her parents left the city of the Golden Gate and journeyed toward the Sierra Nevada Mountains, the highest and steepest in the United States.

"Sierra" means "mountain range" in Spanish, and "Nevada" means "heavy fall of snow." So it is known as the "Snowy Range."

All day they drove along smooth highways and Carmen could not help thinking of Carmencita's trip. Gold mines were now peaceful villages and quiet farms.

"Those golden days of '49 are over," said

Mr. Stevens. "But the Californians still have a golden harvest in their fruit."

Carmen began to wonder about Juan. What had happened to him after that day? Had he been badly hurt? Did he ever play another prank? Had Carmencita's father found gold? Poor little Carmencita!

She sighed and cuddled down in the soft seat. Tonight father would read some more. She closed her eyes.

"We are now going to see the oldest living thing in the whole world," said Mr. Stevens.

"Older than Tia Carmencita?" asked Carmen.

Her father and mother both laughed.

"Much older," answered her mother. "Older than the oldest records of man. "It is called the 'Grizzly Giant.' "

Carmen sat up and looked about her. They were entering a great forest of redwood trees.

"Not really a giant?" she asked.

Courtesy of Yosemite Park, and Curry Co.

THE GRIZZLY GIANT

"Yes, indeed," said Mr. Stevens mysteriously. "Wait and see."

They found themselves surrounded by the

tallest, largest trees Carmen had ever seen.

"What big trees!" she exclaimed.

"That is exactly what they are called," said her father. "This is the famous grove of Big Trees, and here is the Grizzly Giant, the biggest of them all!"

They drove their car right through the center of one of the trees. Then they stopped and walked about in Giantland.

"These redwoods grow nowhere else in the world," said Mr. Stevens.

They decided to stop for the night at Yosemite National Park. Before going to bed, Carmen's father told her the legend of how Yosemite was named.

Once upon a time, a young Indian leader met a savage bear in the forest. The Indian had no weapon with him so he seized the limb of a tree.

A terrible battle took place between the young brave and the wild beast. But, at last, the bear was slain.

Wounded, the Indian crept back to camp, where his people honored him and thereafter called him "Yosemite—Great Grizzly."

This, in time, became the name of his whole tribe and, finally, the name of the valley where they lived.

Yosemite is a wonderland. Waterfalls of fairy colors fall from sky-kissed mountains. The valley seems like puppet-land with monsters of nature towering above it on all sides.

"I feel so small tonight," said Carmen, as she hopped into bed. "Giant trees and mountains! Oh, I am only a little—a little——"

"A little caterpillar," finished her father.

"The caterpillar would like to be read to, please," said Carmen.

Mr. Stevens shook his head. "Not tonight," he answered. "You are tired and the next chapter—well——"

He hesitated.

Courtesy of Yosemite Park, and Curry Co.

YOSEMITE FALLS, YOSEMITE NATIONAL PARK

"What is it, Daddy?" asked Carmen. "Why can't you read it? Have you read it yourself?"

"Yes, I have," answered Mr. Stevens. "And I would rather you heard it by day."

"But why, Daddy?" persisted Carmen.

"Because it . . . oh, I just want you to have a good night's sleep; that's all," he replied.

"Then it's going to be exciting!" cried Carmen, happily.

The next day they left for Lake Tahoe. On the way they passed Donner Lake. A sad and cruel tale surrounds this lovely lake.

In eighteen forty-six the Donner party, men, women and children, came all the way from Illinois. After a trip of many hardships, they finally reached these mountains.

They thought their troubles were over. But, alas, the snow began to fall, and it did not stop for days and days. The Donner party was snowed in. They were not able to

STAR LAKE, TAHOE

move, and were forced to remain on the shores of the lake.

Their provisions gave out. It was bitter cold. Most of these poor people died. Only eighteen of them lived to tell this fearful tale.

Lake Tahoe at last! "Lake of the Sky." "Land of the Sky-Blue Water."

They had already passed through Giant-land and Wonderland. Now they were in "Angel-land." High—so high that angels must surely live here!   At least, so thought Carmen.

All about her she saw straight, tall pine trees. Not a human thing in the deep forests. All was so still.

Then, as they drove along, she noticed someone walking beneath the trees. Ah, some glorious being from the skies!

"Please drive slowly, Daddy," she whispered. "I'm sure it is an angel!"

As the figure came closer, she saw that her "angel" was brown and fat. It was an Indian woman, carrying a huge basket on her head!

Carmen knew that long ago only Indians lived here. There are still quite a few left. They build their camps beneath the trees.

Suddenly Mrs. Stevens gasped. They slowed down and gazed below. They were on a narrow road, between two jewels made of water. One, a shining blue-green gem— Emerald Bay. The other, quiet, solemn, lonely, dark, a sea of mystery—Cascade Lake.

"I think that this is the most beautiful spot I have ever seen," said Mother. And Mother had visited many lands.

"Would you like to see Floating Island?" asked Mr. Stevens.

"I would like to eat some!" laughed Carmen.

"But this is not a dessert," said her father. "It is a real island."

And, sure enough, it was a tiny island floating about on one of Tahoe's smaller lakes.

From the top of snow-covered Mt. Tallac, twenty-one of these lakes can be seen.

They stopped at a hotel built upon the shores of the Lake. On one side Carmen could look at the towering mountains. On the other side she gazed out across Lake Tahoe.

Strips of blue seemed painted upon the surface of the water. But the artist must have run out of blue paint, for suddenly he had smeared on a strip of green.

"Why are there so many shades on the lake, Daddy?" asked Carmen.

Her father answered, "Because of the different depths of water and the reflection of the sky."

Next day they sat upon the veranda of the hotel. Little chipmunks ran all about. They came up and ate nuts from Carmen's hand. Mr. Stevens picked up the cow-book.

"And now, how would you like to visit Carmencita and her friends?" he asked.

Carmen was delighted. The sun glittered upon the lake. A little breeze blew through the sweet-smelling pine trees. A saucy-faced chipmunk jumped upon Mr. Stevens' lap and began to bite at the cow-book.

Mr. Stevens laughed and pulled away the book. He threw the little fellow some nuts. Then he began to read.

CHAPTER X

INDIANS!—YESTERDAY

THIS IS CARMENCITA'S COW-BOOK STORY

Lately we had been hearing so much about Oregon that I seemed to wake up in the mornings with the word ringing in my ears. One day I asked my father what it meant.

He said, "The Oregon Country is the great Northwest, my child. It is the entire territory west of the Rocky Mountains and north of California."

"But why do you and Mr. Estevan talk so much about it?" I asked.

"Because," he answered, "we may soon go there."

I asked no more questions just then for my

*father had to go to work.   But a few eve-
nings later we were all told the news.   We
were to leave the mines.*

*My father and Mr. Estevan had not struck
gold.   But our friend, the covered-wagon-
man, had.   He was going back to his home
in Oregon and he offered to take us along in
his wagon.*

*"I am an old pioneer," he said.   "I was one
who helped to conquer and settle the Northwest.   I am going back to the town of Portland in Oregon."*

*"What shall you do there?" asked Mr. Es-
tevan.*

*"California needs food and supplies," he
answered.   "The North is very busy shipping
things to the golden state.   That is a good
business for me."*

*"But what can we do?" asked my father.
"We are poor and we have our children to
support."*

"You have been ranchers," replied our

friend. "Why do you not go far North, take some land and work it?"

Juan had been listening intently. Now he jumped up angrily and stood before the man with his eyes flashing.

"My father would not take land!" he cried. "He is not a thief!"

Mr. Covered-Wagon-Man laughed. "Oh, no, no!" he said. "That is not what I meant. You see, the Government will give land to anyone who is willing to clear it and live on it."

That was enough for my father and Mr. Estevan. They were very tired of being miners. They were very glad to leave. Besides, our Oregon friend told us about the fine schools in the North.

Every evening we listened while he told us tales of this splendid Oregon Country.

The one I liked best was about two brave men, Captain Meriwether Lewis and Lieutenant William Clark. They started from

"MY FATHER IS NOT A THIEF!"

St. Louis in 1804 and crossed the Rocky
Mountains into this vast, unknown land of
Oregon.

They braved the dangers of the wilderness and were attacked by war-like Indians.

But they finally returned safely to St. Louis. This famous trip gave the United States a claim to the Oregon Country.

We also heard the story of how Oregon began. John Jacob Astor founded the Pacific Fur Company and named the settlement Astoria. At the time of his death, John Jacob Astor was the richest man in America.

The stories I did not like to hear, however, were those about Indian attacks. Travellers, returning from the mines, were often murdered by war-like tribes.

"We must travel through the very country where these terrible things are happening," I said to Juan.

But he seemed to enjoy the idea. Dangers meant nothing to Juan if they spelled adventure.

But, oh, I did not want to go. And neither did Hipolito. Not because he was afraid. He just did not like new countries and hard work. He longed always for the rancho.

Juan began to talk nothing but Indians. One night he woke me up war-whooping in his sleep! He asked Mr. Covered-Wagon-Man so many questions that it made me dizzy.

Juan had behaved better since that day when he had painted yellow rocks to fool Hipolito and me. He had been very ill afterwards and I had nursed him.

I had made him promise not to play pranks any more. Every time his head ached he would promise faithfully. But when he felt better I would see that sparkle in his eye and wonder how long he could keep his word!

We left at last, in the covered wagon with our friends. On to Oregon! Oh, those days of weary travel over mountains and across plains!

There were happy moments, of course, and such beautiful scenery. But most of the time was spent in hard work and dreading an Indian attack.

How the men struggled with that wagon! Though the trail was fairly well traveled, we came upon many difficult places.

One night we camped beneath a big, flat rock. I felt sure that Indians lurked up there, watching us, waiting to swoop down upon us!

But my fears were in vain. We were not disturbed. In fact, we were very fortunate on that trip.

We arrived safely at Portland. Here we said good-bye to our friends and found another party going further north.

I should have liked to stay longer in the village of Portland. Boats were piled high with supplies to be sent to the mines. Lumber mills hummed all day long.

I did not want to leave a place where people were living all together to go into a lonely wilderness. For, that is where we were going—to a place called Puget Sound.

Of course we did not know that here, some

day, the great city of Seattle would stand.
Nor did we know that we were on our way
to the state of Washington. At that time, it
was just part of the Oregon Country.

Puget Sound was known to welcome the
new settler. That is why we were going
there. But the Indians did not welcome new
people who came and took the land. They
felt that it belonged to them.

Our new home was only a dense forest.
But we were so glad to stop travelling that
it did not matter. Besides, this was a beau-
tiful land.

We built our cabin deep in the woods. A
saw mill not far away buzzed and buzzed.
Near by, in the sound, lay a great battleship.

Father and Mr. Estevan immediately be-
gan to work the land. Hipolito helped them.
Juan and I went to school—a log school-
house in the woods.

We studied with children from the other
settlements. They had all come from far-

away places. It was interesting to hear them talk. Juan and I said little for we felt shy about speaking English.

All was going so well that we really thought our troubles were at an end.

Even Juan had done nothing very terrible lately. Of course, he had once been found on the battleship when we had searched for him all day.

And again he had gone Indian scouting and come back with the seat of his trousers torn off. He had not met Indians, but he had disturbed a watch dog guarding his owner's cabin!

And then came that awful night! We were all so happy, sitting before our roaring fire. Mr. Estevan was strumming on the guitar. Juan was singing a gay Spanish song. I was dancing, my father and Hipolito swaying to the music. It was almost like old rancho days.

But, all at once, we paused in our gayety

I WAS DANCING

and listened. Out of the woods came far-
away cries—terrible, shrill cries! Closer
and closer!

"An Indian attack!"

My father and Mr. Estevan jumped to their feet.

"Bar all windows and doors! Bring the guns!"

It had come! The attack which I had been dreading! So far, I had seen only peaceful Indians. But those now rushing toward our cabin would be war-crazed, smeared with grease, yelling, and shooting guns!

"Oh, Father!" I cried, and ran to his side. I clasped his knees and sobbed.

"Come, my darling," he said.

He lifted me up in one arm. In the other he held his gun. The piercing shrieks were coming closer. Soon the forest was alive with them. They were the most horrible yells I have ever heard.

My father, Mr. Estevan, Hipolito and Juan crouched beneath the windows, and loaded their guns. I crept up close to my father. I heard the Redskins outside our cabin. I thought the noise would deafen me.

Added to the screams, came shooting of bullets against the house. A window shutter suddenly crashed, and I saw Juan's head pop up and thrust itself through the hole.

"Down!" bellowed my father. "Do you want your head shot off?"

The answer was a "whiz" from a bullet which flew over Juan's head. It struck a picture on the opposite wall and smashed it to bits.

Down bobbed Juan's head. But "pop! pop!" went his gun through the hole. This time they had given him a real gun—one that would shoot!

"Let me help, too, Father," I said.

But he told me to cuddle down beside him and not to move.

The cabin filled with smoke.

"We cannot hold out very much longer," said Mr. Estevan. "If only we could get word to the troops on the battleship!"

But how could we do that?

Big splinters began to fall out of the cabin walls. How much longer would it be? My father covered me with his coat. For hours and hours I seemed to hear the "bang! bang! eeeooooo! Crash!"

Another window smashed!

Then, all at once, silence! What had happened? I peeked out from under the coat. Smoke stung my eyes. Father and Mr. Estevan still crouched, but they were not shooting. They were listening.

The noise had really stopped. We looked out cautiously. The Indians were gone!

Suddenly Hipolito gave a shout, "See! The troops are coming!"

My heart beat fast. I turned to Juan to see the joy in his face. Juan was not there! I felt cold all over.

"Father—" I began.

But before I could say another word, Juan burst into the room, waving a flag and yelling more loudly than any Indian!

"The troops!" he screamed. His voice was hoarse with yelling. "They've chased the Injuns away! Hoorah for the United States flag! Hoorah for President Fillmore! Hurrah for Juan Estevan!"

Then he did an Indian war dance all over the room.

Sure enough, the Redskins had seen the troops coming and that is why they had disappeared.

But how had the troops happened to come to our aid? How had they known of our trouble? Ah, that is my favorite part of the story. Our own brave little Juan had brought them!

In the back part of the house there was a small door which led out to the wood-shed. Juan had gone out through this door, crawled to the wood-shed and crept stealthily through the bushes.

Skirting those shrieking savages, and their spitting guns, he had then made a dash to the battleship and brought the troops to our aid.

Do you think Juan became a hero? You should have seen how we spoiled him. Even the troops did. They took him on board their ship next day and treated him like a king. They made him their mascot.

Oh, we were very proud of Juan. But I think I was the proudest of all—except, perhaps, Juan himself!

CHAPTER XI

THE BEAVER STATE—TODAY

What a difference between the wild yesterday of Carmencita and the well-ordered today of Carmen Stevens!

Carmen found the Oregon Country now neatly divided into the two states of Oregon and Washington.

Some say that the name "Oregon" comes from the Spanish word, "oregones," meaning "big-eared men." Others prefer to think that it is taken from the Spanish "Aura Agua," meaning "gently falling waters." The rain loves to visit this land of Oregon.

"Busy as a beaver" is an old saying, and Oregon is the Beaver State. A beaver builds and works, and so does Oregon. She is busy

CRATER LAKE, OREGON

ship-building, fishing, farming, fruit growing, and cattle raising.

Carmen and her family motored to Crater Lake, a spot of rare beauty.

"This lake was once a volcano, a fire-mountain," explained Mr. Stevens. "It is probably the deepest lake in the United States."

"Oh, look, Daddy!" cried Carmen. "There

is a big sailing ship out there on the lake!"

Mr. Stevens answered, "It is not a ship, but only a mass of rock. It is called 'The Phantom Ship' because others besides you have been deceived."

There were still more curious shapes formed by the grey lava around the lake.

Between the states of Oregon and Washington flows the Columbia River. It is famous for its glorious scenery and for its salmon.

The Columbia River is called "The Great River of the West." Near its mouth stands Cape Disappointment, named by disappointed English and Spanish explorers, seeking the Columbia River.

An American, Captain Robert Grey, found the great river and named it in honor of his ship, "Columbia."

Carmen's father stopped the car on the highway above a deep canyon near some salmon fisheries.

"Now I am going to tell you a true fairy story," said he.

Carmen gave him a puzzled look. Mrs. Stevens laughed.

"That is like saying a 'hot snow-ball' or a 'dry swim,'" she told her husband. "I have never heard of a 'true' fairy story, and neither has Carmen."

"Have you ever heard of flying fish?" asked Mr. Stevens.

"Yes," laughed Carmen. "And I've heard of singing giraffes and . . . and all kinds of things that are not true!"

"But now you are going to see real flying fish," said Mr. Stevens.

Then he told the strange tale of the salmon who is born and dies in fresh water, but grows up in the salt sea.

Mrs. Salmon battles her way upstream to shallow places where she likes to lay her eggs. When falls or rapids try to bar her way she calmly leaps over them. Nothing

Courtesy of Portland Chamber of Commerce
HAULING IN ROYAL CHINOOK SALMON

can stop these determined sea-folk. And
that is why we hear about the "leaping
salmon" or "flying fish."

After the eggs are hatched, the parent
salmon drift down to the sea again. But
they die on the way. Baby Salmon soon
hears the call of the sea and downstream he
goes. The lazy little fellow floats backwards

Courtesy of Portland Chamber of Commerce
PORTLAND, OREGON, WITH MT. HOOD IN THE BACKGROUND

and lets food from the water fall into his mouth.

The Stevens' were now nearing what used to be the old "Oregon Trail." Over it came explorers, Indians, gold seekers.

"It was a pity that Carmencita's father and Mr. Estevan did not strike gold," said Carmen.

"But they did," said Mr. Stevens. "That is, Juan did, later on. You see, the Oregon Country had a gold rush, too. Juan was then grown up and he became a miner."

"Oh, don't tell me any more," said Carmen. "But read it to me this evening."

As they entered Portland, Carmen exclaimed, "But, Daddy, this is not a little village!"

"It certainly is not," answered Mr. Stevens. "Portland is Oregon's largest city. The California gold rush started her growth. Today she is an important center."

"She is a flower garden!" cried Mrs. Stevens enthusiastically.

Every year Portland covers herself with flowers and celebrates. Carmen had arrived at this eventful time. She watched nearly one hundred gay floats, made of blossoms, parade down the streets.

She watched thousands of school children, decked in roses, dancing and playing. The

perfume of flowers filled the air. Beautiful
Mt. Hood in her snow-capped glory, stood
over the scene, which was almost too lovely
to be real.

"This should be called Rose City instead
of Portland, " said Carmen.

"That is just what it is often called," said
her father.

Then he told her the story of how Portland was named. Two early settlers were
arguing one day.

"The town shall be named Boston," said
one, who came from Boston, Massachusetts.

"No, I say it shall be Portland," insisted
the other, who hailed from Portland, Maine.

"Let us toss a coin," suggested the Boston
man, "and I shall bet on tails to win."

They tossed the coin, but heads won.

In the hotel that evening Carmen un-
packed the cow-book. The trip had been
hot and Carmen noticed that the cow-book's
jacket had come loose.

She began to pick at it and her finger touched a loose paper inside the binding. She pulled it half-way out. It was a sheet of paper with Spanish writing on it. In large letters she noticed the word, "expediente."

But, at that moment, her father came into the room. She hurriedly stuffed back the paper and pressed down the hide jacket.

"Carmen!" scolded her father. "You are destroying that precious old book! Shame! Children of today have no respect!"

He took the cow-book from her and began to read.

She listened to the story of how Carmencita and her friends grew up in the Oregon Country; how lazy Hipolito went back to California. He married an American girl and they became Carmen Stevens' great-grandfather and great-grandmother.

Juan went to the Oregon mines and struck gold. Then he married Carmencita and they became Carmen's great grand-uncle

"SHAME!" HE SCOLDED

Juan and her great grand-Aunt, Carmencita.

"It seems funny to think of little Juan as a great grand-uncle," said Carmen. "What happened to him, Daddy?"

"Juan Estevan died many years ago," answered her father. "With the gold rush to Alaska, Seattle became an important shipping center. At this time many people again set forth to make their fortunes, and among them Juan.

"Though he was then an old man, Juan could not resist excitement and adventure. But this time he did not survive the hardships. He passed away in Alaska."

"Poor Tia Carmencita!" sighed Carmen. "She must have felt very sad. She always loved him so much. Even when they were little and Juan played pranks and made her anxious."

"She still lives in the old house which he built for her in Seattle," said Mr. Stevens. "That is where we shall be tomorrow and where we are going to live."

"But I am sure Tia will never forget those days on her rancho," said Carmen. "Oh, I wish she could go back there once more. Because it really still belongs to her, doesn't it, Daddy?"

"If her father owned a land grant, then surely it does," answered Mr. Stevens. "But unless the land grant were to be found, nobody could prove it."

That night Carmen lay awake in bed, thinking. She was glad to go to Seattle, of course. But, oh, how wonderful it would be if they could all live on that beautiful old rancho!

What could have become of that land grant?

She began to doze off. Into her sleepy mind came her father's scolding when he had found her picking at the cow-book. It made her feel ashamed. "Destroying that precious book! Children of today have no respect!"

What was that loose paper inside the jacket of the cow-book? She had just had time to notice a strange seal and Spanish

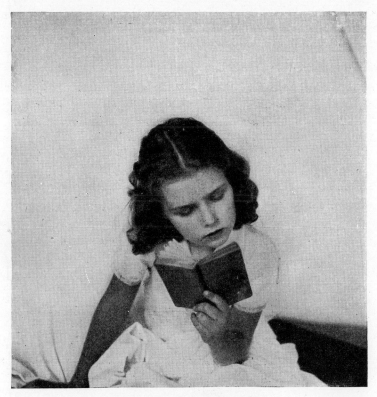

SHE LOOKED UP THE WORD

writing. She remembered the word that had stood out so boldly. "expediente."

Where had she heard that word before? It sounded so familiar. She kept the little

Spanish dictionary beside her bed. She had looked up many words for her father and now she switched on the light and looked up the word, "expediente."

The dictionary told her that it meant—"a writing issued from public offices——"

Why, her father had once explained to her that a paper given by a public office was a "grant." Could "expediente" mean the same thing? Could——

Carmen sat up in bed with a sudden start. Could it mean that she, Carmen Stevens, had found the grant to the Estevan Rancho?

This paper inside the jacket of the cow-book had on it a seal and a word that meant "grant."

Carmen felt her cheeks begin to burn with excitement. She must look inside the cow-book again. At once!

But Daddy had taken it into his room. She would steal in there now.

Trembling, she took up her kimono from

a near-by chair. She was so excited that she started to put her feet through the sleeves!

Daddy and Mother must not hear her taking the cow-book. They would not understand and she could not tell them until she made sure. They might laugh at her.

She tiptoed into her parents' room. She tried to be very quiet and felt her way cautiously in the dark.

Bang! Oh, dear! Why did that old suitcase have to be sticking out so far!

"Who is there?" cried Daddy.

"It . . . it's only C . . . Carmen," she shivered.

"What do you want, Carmen?" he asked.

"I . . . I wanted . . . well, now I don't want it. Good-night, D . . . Daddy!"

She scurried away like a frightened little mouse, leaving bewildered parents behind.

CHAPTER XII

THE EVERGREEN STATE—TODAY

Washington—the Evergreen State! The leading lumber state! The leading apple state! The leading wild game state!

Western Washington is lumber land. Lumber means forests, forests mean trees, and trees mean beauty.

Carmen and her parents motored along scenic highways. Glorious pictures of nature on all sides made each hour of their trip more interesting than the last.

Besides the highways, there are many fine railways in Washington. But the first railroad was not so fine. It was known as the "Rawhide Railroad." The rails were made of wood covered with rawhide.

148

Often hungry wolves came down from the hills and ate up the rawhide. Imagine having your train tracks eaten up! It delayed trains and was most annoying.

A strange custom in those days was to have a collie dog sitting upon the cow-catcher of the engine. The collie's task was to drive cattle off the tracks.

Washington might be called a State of Nations. This is the reason why:

Along the coast, near a place called Aberdeen (which is a Scotch name) is a settlement of Finnish people. They raise fine cranberries and they are American citizens. But they still love the dances and games of their native country, Finland.

Then, if you should go to Whatcom County you would find a colony of Dutch people— wooden shoes, tulips and all! It is known as the "Holland of America" and Bellingham is called "Tulip City."

There are still many Indians to be found

in Washington. Excellent schools have been built for the young Hiawathas.

"Here we are in New York!" said Mr. Stevens. He said it quite seriously, too.

Carmen looked at her father in astonishment. Had he suddenly lost his wits? Why, New York was far, far away in the East, while they were far, far out in the West! They were driving through the streets of Seattle.

"Yes, New York," repeated Mr. Stevens. "When Seattle was first settled, some people from New York gave it that name. Other settlers laughed at them and called the town 'New York—Alki,' which meant 'New York —by and by' in Indian language."

"How did it happen to be named Seattle?" asked Carmen.

"That was the name of a friendly Indian chief," said her father.

Carmen wanted to see the spot in the forest where Carmencita's hut had stood.

Mr. Stevens stopped the car on a crowded city street.

"It might have stood about here," he said.

No wonder Carmen was astonished. Such a short time ago this modern city had been a wild forest! Indians had attacked settlers and nobody had known anything about airplanes, radios and telephones.

Seattle is now the largest city of the Pacific Northwest. Hills with pretty homes upon them rise above her busy streets.

The State of Washington is rich in electrical power. So Seattle is one of the best lighted cities in the world.

She has miles and miles of harbor where boats come and go from and to all parts of the world. It is the gateway to Alaska and the Orient.

The Pike Place Market is full of color and busy sounds. Here, again, are people of many nations.

"See the little Japanese girl selling goldfish," said Carmen, "from Japan, I guess."

"And the Indians with their beads and baskets," added her mother.

Mr. Stevens drove to Capitol Hill in the center of Seattle and stopped the car.

"Now let us look down upon the 'city that was once forest,' " he said.

"And up at the 'Mountain That Was God,' " said Mrs. Stevens.

Carmen wanted to know why her mother called beautiful Mt. Rainier "The Mountain That Was God."

"Because that is the name given it by the Indians," explained Mrs. Stevens. "Mt. Rainier was once much higher than it is to-day. But they say that it erupted and four thousand feet of the peak blew off."

"Where did the pieces fall?" asked Carmen.

"They scattered all over Puget Sound and became part of the soil," her mother answered.

MT. RAINIER NATIONAL PARK

"Mt. Rainier is called 'Mt. Tacoma' by the people of Tacoma and 'Rainier' by those of Seattle," Mrs. Stevens continued. "But whatever name it goes by, it is still a wonder mountain, the tallest in the United States that is always covered with snow."

"Some day," Mr. Stevens suggested, "we

will visit Mt. Rainier National Park and see
the curious caverns carved from ice, and
climb all the way up to the top!"

Mrs. Stevens sighed. "Oh, dear!" she
said. "It makes me tired just to hear of such
a thing!"

As they drove up to Tia's door, Carmen's
heart began to beat fast. At last she was
going to see her travelling companion of the
Golden Coast! Little Carmencita!

But just as exciting to Carmen was a plan
she had formed. For, in spite of all that she
had seen that day, she had not forgotten the
cow-book and what it contained.

So she planned that as soon as they arrived at Tia's house, she would take the cow-
book and pick off its hide jacket! Yes, she
would show no respect at all and her
father could scold if he liked. But, Carmen
knew that if she found what she was looking
for, he would not scold!

Tia's house was old fashioned but comfortable. The little old lady greeted them in her sitting room. She was tiny and frail, but, thought Carmen, so beautiful!

She wore a lace cap over her white hair, and a demure grey gown. She had about her shoulders a Spanish shawl. She took Carmen's hand in hers. When she spoke her voice was soft and she had a Spanish accent.

"So happee I am to see you, Carmen mio," she said. "We have make the same treep—you an' me. You mus' tell me about yours, eh? I have tell you already about mine in the cow-book."

"Our trip was not nearly so exciting as yours," said Carmen. "There were no bandits, or Indians, or—or Juans! Oh, I wish I could have been with you!"

"Ah, no, child!" laughed Tia. "You mus' be glad you are not! An' some day I tell you more about it."

"Will you tell me more about the rancho?"

asked Carmen. "I have been there and seen it and I love it as much as you do."

At the word "rancho" a sad look came over Tia's face. Carmen put her arm about the old lady's shoulder.

"I felt so sorry when your father lost it," she added.

"I shall never forget my so beautiful home in California," said Tia wistfully.

The travellers were shown to their rooms. The first thing Carmen did was to ask her father for the cow-book. Mr. Stevens opened his suitcase, but the cow-book was not there!

"I was sure that I packed it last night," he said. "But it certainly is not here now."

Carmen's eyes grew big with fear.

"But, Daddy, we *must* find it! We must!" she cried.

"Yes, of course," agreed Mr. Stevens. "We must not lose that fine old souvenir."

Fine old souvenir indeed! Oh, thought

Carmen, if Daddy only knew what else might be lost! The precious Spanish grant to the rancho!

Carmen now felt certain that what she had seen was truly the grant. But had she found it only to lose it again?

A great lump came into her throat. Mr. Stevens turned his suitcase inside out and upside down. But no cow-book!

"I shall write to the Portland hotel," he said.

All sorts of terrible ideas came into Carmen's head. Perhaps a spy had heard about the grant and had stolen the cow-book. Oh, she would never see it again! Never!

And just then she did see it! For her mother walked into the room holding it in her hand!

"Here is your book, Carmen," said Mrs. Stevens. "I packed it in my bag, for I found it lying on the floor this morning after Daddy's bag was packed."

THERE IT WAS!

Suddenly, a cyclone leaped up and kissed Mrs. Stevens! Then the cyclone, which was Carmen, disappeared into her room as fast as she could go. She locked her door and then deliberately peeled off the hide jacket of the cow-book.

There it was! All through those many

years, the grant had lain in the same cozy nest where that rascally Yankee had put it. The rightful claim to the property of Carmencita Estevan!

Can you imagine what happened when Carmen showed her wonderful discovery to her family? Can you see the joy in the face of little old Tia?

Mr. Stevens told them that he would have to consult a lawyer and that it might take a long time before they could expect to win back their rancho. But, with the help of Carmencita's cow-book story, he hoped to prove that the land still belonged to her.

So good-bye, Tia Carmencita—and may you soon see your beloved rancho again!

Good-bye, Mr. Stevens—and may you help Tia in her desire to live once more in the land of her memories.

Good-bye, Mrs. Stevens—and perhaps you will forget your illnesses when you listen to Tia's tales of her rugged youth.

Good-bye, Carmen.   You have already forgotten Betty-next-door.   And your face will
never look like this any more ☹, but always
like this ☺.

And why not?   You are a fortunate little
girl to be living in this comfortable, modern
day, on the beautiful Golden Coast!

THE END